To my family, the authors
of our wonderful life.

Requests for permission to make copies of any part of the work should be submitted online at info@mascotbooks.com or mailed to Mascot Books, 560 Herndon Parkway #120, Herndon, VA 20170.

PRT0712A

Printed in the United States

ISBN-13: 9781937406424
ISBN-10: 1937406423

www.mascotbooks.com

Hello, Big Red!

Heather Little

Illustrated by Tim Williams

It was a beautiful fall day at Cornell.
Big Red Bear had plans to meet his friends
later at the hockey match.

Big Red Bear stopped at Collegetown Bagels.
Students there for breakfast said,

"Hello, Big Red!"

Big Red Bear shouted down Cascadilla Gorge,

"Go, Big Red!"

He listened for his echo to return from far below.

Big Red Bear made the long climb
up Libe Slope. Crew members on
Cayuga Lake yelled out,

"Hello, Big Red!"

Big Red Bear walked up Ho Plaza and stopped at Louie's Lunch for a sub. Louie said, "Here's your favorite made to go, Big Red!"

A family at McGraw Clocktower listened to the chimes and said, "Hello, Big Red!" Big Red Bear still wondered how that pumpkin appeared at the top of the steeple one cold October morning.

If the statues of Ezra Cornell and Andrew White saw how it got there, they were not telling. Big Red Bear was still hungry, so he went for some Clocktower Pumpkin ice cream at the Cornell Dairy.

Big Red Bear was excited to get to the
match and took a shortcut through Uris
Library. The librarian whispered,
"Hello, Big Red."

Tim Williams

Alumni at Willard Straight Hall remembered
Big Red from their time at Cornell.

The a capella groups huddled together
and sang out, "Hello again, Big Red!"

Former students had returned to Sage Chapel to get married. The bride and groom smiled for a picture with Big Red Bear.

Big Red Bear hurried through the Veterinary College.
All the animals were glad to see him and said,
"Woof-woof! Me-ow! Chirp-chirp!" All of that really
meant, "Hello, Big Red!"

Big Red Bear ran by Schoellkopf Field, Friedman Center, and Newman Arena. Team members and band members waved and called, "Hello, Big Red!"

Big Red Bear finally reached Lynah Rink. The
crowd stood for the "Star Spangled Banner"
and sang his name extra loud! The players
took to the ice.

The arena was full of excitement as the team scored a goal. They were headed for another victory. Big Red Bear and his friends cheered for all the action and Cornell won the match!

It was dark when the hockey match was over. Students of Blue Light Escort Service asked, "Where do you want to go, Big Red?" and walked him home.

Triphammer Falls would soon drip icicles
into Fall Creek again. While all of his bear
friends were hibernating,

Big Red Bear would be busy enjoying
the fall and winter activities.

Spring would bring the excitement of Dragon
Day and lots of music on Slope Day.

The plantations would be in
full bloom.

Big Red Bear shivered as he snuggled
under the covers. He needed his rest to
be ready for it all. Good-night, Big Red!

Heather is a medical transcriptionist who lives with her husband, Jim in Altoona, Pennsylvania.